To Keith Lloyd - a very good friend to gorillas

Text copyright © Jill Jago
Illustrations copyright © Gerry Livingston

First published in 1995

First published in Great Britain in 1995
Reprinted in 1996 by Macdonald Young Books
61 Western Road
Hove
East Sussex
BN3 1JD

The right of Jill Jago to be identified as the author of
this Work and the right of Gerry Livingston to be identified as
the illustrator of this Work has been asserted by them in accordance
with the Copyright, Designs and Patents Act 1988.

Printed and bound in Belgium by Proost International Book Co.

British Library Cataloguing in Publication Data available.

ISBN: 0 7500 1660 4
ISBN: 0 7500 1661 2 (pb)

KIJO
the Baby Gorilla

by
Jill Jago & Gerry Livingston

MACDONALD YOUNG BOOKS

Kijo the baby gorilla lives in the big dark African forest. When his mother goes looking for berries and fruit to eat, Kijo always goes with her. He clings tight to the thick fur on her back.

Kijo loves playing hide-and-seek with his brother and sister, round and round among the tall trees and thick ferns.
Life in the forest is fun!

While the young gorillas play,
the father gorilla keeps watch.
Suddenly he smells danger.

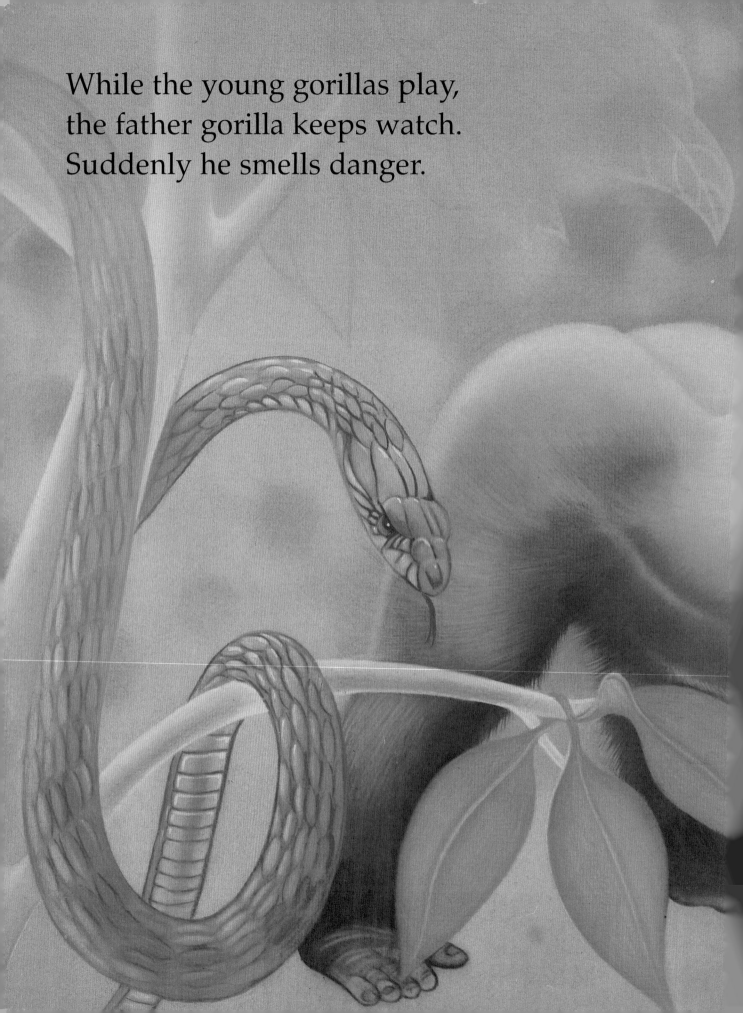

Men!
They are coming closer and closer,
hunting for gorillas.
Father gorilla beats his chest and roars.

WRAAGGHH!

Quick, quick Kijo!
Father gorilla races away with the little ones,
into the thickest part of the forest,
where the men cannot find them.

At last Kijo's father decides it is safe to stop.
But Kijo cannot see his mother anywhere.
Where is she? What will he do without
the warm comfort of her fur?

Kijo creeps off to look for his lost mother.

Who's this?

It's only a pangolin, Kijo!
A pangolin won't harm a baby gorilla.

Rustle, rustle.

The noise in the bushes makes Kijo jump.
But it's just a tiny antelope. She prances
towards him and runs away again.
She is far more frightened than Kijo.

Kijo hears another noise in the grass.
Something is creeping closer and closer . . .

It's a leopard! She's looking for something tasty to give her hungry cubs for supper.

Run, Kijo! Run!

Kijo is too scared to move.
The leopard is ready to spring.
Suddenly she pricks up her ears.
Her cubs are calling her.
With a snarl, she turns and bounds away.

Poor little Kijo is shaking with fright.
He is lost and very hungry, and he
needs his mother to protect him.
But Kijo is so tired. He just curls up
in a sad little ball and goes to sleep.

He sleeps for a long time until …

... someone wakes him.

It's a big gorilla - is she his mother?
No, she smells different. She knows
Kijo isn't her baby, and she walks away.

Kijo begins to whimper . . .

. . . and the big gorilla comes back.
Very gently, she picks Kijo up and
cradles him in her arms.
She has found a new baby.
And Kijo has found a new mother.

What do you know about gorillas?

Young gorillas and chimps are more like us than any other animals. They use their hands in the same ways as we do - to put food in their mouths and to make things.

A baby gorilla is not likely to survive if it loses its mother, but this often happens in the African forests. Hunters and poachers kill gorillas to eat or to sell as souvenirs.

Now more and more trees are being chopped down to clear the way for new roads and towns or to provide wood for furniture and other things. The forests are disappearing and soon there may be nowhere for gorilla families to live.

Luckily they have many friends who care what happens to them.